Naomi Nash

Problems
at the
Pond

by Jessica Lee Anderson

illustrated by Alejandra Barajas

PICTURE WINDOW BOOKS
a capstone imprint

Published by Picture Window Books, an imprint of Capstone.
1710 Roe Crest Drive, North Mankato, Minnesota 56003
capstonepub.com

Text copyright © 2023 by Jessica Lee Anderson
Illustrations copyright © 2023 by Capstone

Library of Congress Cataloging-in-Publication Data is available
on the Library of Congress website.

ISBN: 9781666349429 (hardcover)
ISBN: 9781666349467 (paperback)
ISBN: 9781666349504 (ebook PDF)

Summary: When Naomi hears about a snake causing trouble at a nearby
pond, she dismisses it—at first. After all, a pond is a natural place, and
snakes aren't mean. They're just snakes. But the reports keep coming.
The snake-saving club decides to investigate. It's up to them to solve
the mystery of the "mean" snake before someone gets hurt.

Designed by Kay Fraser & Jaime Willems

All internet sites appearing in back matter were available and accurate
when this book was sent to press.

Printed and bound in the USA. PO# 5195

TABLE OF CONTENTS

CHAPTER 1

PHONE CALLS

Snake fact #1: "Gravid" means a snake is pregnant or full of eggs.

Ringgggg! Our home phone rang bright and early Saturday morning—before breakfast even.

"It's too early for a phone call!" my older brother, Nolan, complained. He let go of the book he was reading and covered his ears.

It *was* early. But ever since we—along with my best friend, Emma—had started a snake rescue club, we'd been getting lots of phone calls.

I dashed for the phone. A snake or some critter might've needed our help. That was the whole reason we'd started our club.

Will this be a real call or another prank? I wondered as I picked up the phone in the living room.

Someone yesterday had been rude. They'd said our snake rescue club was a waste of time because snakes aren't worth saving. I'd tried to

explain that snakes play an important part in nature, but the caller had hung up on me.

"Good morning," I said. I crossed my fingers that this would be a good call.

"Hi, dear. I'm looking for the snake club," a woman's voice said. She spoke slowly, and her voice was kind of shaky.

"You found us!" I said. "How can we help you?"

"My husband and I were on a morning stroll when we came across a good-sized turtle out in the street. In the street! Can you believe that?" she asked.

Nolan had said before that I sometimes sounded like a know-it-all, so I thought of a kind reply.

"Yes, ma'am. Sometimes, turtles will cross roads to look for food and water. Maybe even a place to build a nest."

"Oh? Like to have babies?" the woman asked. It was a little hard to hear her because

Dad had started blending something in the kitchen.

"Yep. Turtles dig nests to lay their eggs. Baby turtles develop inside the eggs and then hatch," I explained. I had to raise my voice a bit over the noise of the blender.

"Fascinating," the woman said.

I could talk about reptiles all day, but I figured that wasn't why this woman had called.

"Is the turtle in some kind of trouble?" I asked.

The woman's voice softened, like she was smiling. "Oh, not at all! My husband and I took it to a nearby pond. We didn't want it to get run over by a car or a biker not paying attention."

"Thanks for looking out for the turtle!" I said. It was nice to know there were people out there willing to help. "That's the goal of our club."

If we'd been talking in person, I would've held up the logo Emma had designed. *WE HELP SNAKES. WE HELP PEOPLE. WE HELP OUR NEIGHBORHOOD.*

The woman's voice still sounded like she was smiling. "It's a wonderful thing you children are doing! Anyway, the reason I called is because of a snake we saw at the pond. It was mean and aggressive. I was afraid it was going to bite my husband when he released the turtle."

Snake fact number twenty-one, I thought. *Snakes might react if someone bothers or surprises them, but they aren't aggressive.*

I'd been writing down snake facts in my notebook for as long as I could remember. They always came in handy.

"That's strange," I said. "Snakes usually like to stay away from people. Do you think it got startled?"

The woman's voice sounded more serious now. "I suppose it's possible. But I thought I should warn others to protect people at the pond. You have an adult take care of this case, though, okay? It could be a water moccasin."

Some people couldn't tell the difference between venomous and nonvenomous water snakes. It made me think of snake fact #82: *Northern cottonmouths are pit vipers known as water moccasins—the only kind of venomous water snake in North America.*

I wanted to share the fact, but I also wanted to get off the phone to eat breakfast. "I'll let my parents know. They're trained wildlife rehabilitators. Thank you for helping the turtle and for telling us about the snake."

I hung up just as Dad shouted, "Smoothies are ready!"

Nolan and I joined him at the kitchen table. Mom was a veterinarian and had left for work before I even woke up. Saturdays were busy at the Austin Exotic Animal Hospital.

"What flavor is this—chunky?" Nolan asked. He inspected his yellow-orangish glass of smoothie before taking a sip.

I did the same. The smoothie was good, though not as good as Dad's baking. He did most of the cooking for our family and made most things from scratch.

"It's a tropical oatmeal smoothie. Breakfast you can drink," Dad explained. "Tell us about the phone call, Naomi."

The smoothie turned out to be too thick for a straw, so I used a spoon instead. I got brain freeze! As soon as it went away, I told Dad and Nolan about how the couple had rescued a turtle.

"The lady said they came across an aggressive snake at a nearby pond. Some people think snakes are mean because of the way they look—"

Nolan cut me off. "Yeah, especially cottonmouths with that ridge above their

eyes. It makes them look angry, like this."
He furrowed his brows and scowled.

Nolan looked so silly I almost snorted my
smoothie out of my nose. My brother had sure
learned a lot about snakes since we'd started
our club.

Dad slurped down the rest of his smoothie.
"I liked trying something new, but I think I'll
stick with baking," he said to himself.

"I'll take whatever I can eat . . . or drink!" Nolan said, finishing his smoothie.

"Agreed," I said. Just then the phone started ringing again.

Nolan groaned. "Who's calling now? It's barely eight-thirty!"

I raced to answer the phone. "It's probably Emma. We planned on hanging out this morning."

But when I answered, a surprise waited for me on the other end of the line.

CHAPTER 2

ALIEN ANTENNA

Snake fact #2: Most snakes lay eggs, but some give birth to live babies the same way that mammals do.

"Uh, hi," a woman said. She sounded younger than the first caller. "My name is Thuy. My friend passed along this number and said your club might be able to help. . . ."

I perked up. I hoped this wasn't a prank. "What's the problem?" I asked.

"Well," the woman said, "there's some kind of creature on my back porch."

"What kind of creature?" I asked.

I knew our club would be happy to help as long as it wasn't a venomous snake. The police or a professional snake remover would have to help with that.

"Honestly, I have no idea what it is!" Thuy said. "I can send a picture."

"Hold on, please." I turned toward the kitchen and covered the phone with my hand. "Dad, can you come here?"

"Sure." Dad walked over and took the phone. He listened for a minute, then said, "How about you email me the photo? I'll call you back once we've had a chance to take a look at the creature."

After rattling off his email address, Dad hung up, then went over to the computer in the living room.

"What do we have here?" he asked, pulling up his email.

Nolan joined us at the computer, breathing over my shoulder as we looked at the computer screen. Dad scratched his head and turned sideways to get a better look. I did the same.

The picture was dark and kind of blurry. But something was clearly trapped in a dark gap where the house ended and the patio began. It had a weird-looking center and two long things sticking up.

What in the world is that? I wondered.

"Is it a miniature alien or something?" Nolan asked. He moved in for a closer look.

I turned my head the other way. I could see what he meant.

"Do you think those two things sticking up are antenna or legs?" I asked.

Dad tilted his head to the other side too. "This is like one of those brain puzzles. Possibly legs?"

Nolan laughed. "I vote alien antenna."

I pointed to what I thought were webbed feet. "It sort of looks like an upside-down amphibian. A frog might be stuck in the crack by the patio. If it is, we could pluck it out. Can we go investigate, Dad?"

Dad shut off the computer. "Sure, I'm curious too. I'll call Thuy back. But I have to admit, I'm a little worried."

"Why?" Nolan and I asked at the same time. Dad hardly ever seemed worried.

"Can you imagine how you famous you two will be if this thing really does turn out to be an alien species?" Dad said, chuckling to himself.

I relaxed. "I bet it's a frog. Thanks, Dad!"

Dad called Thuy to get the details about where we needed to go. While he did that, I checked in with Emma. I knew she wouldn't want to miss this.

"Ready to work on the club?" Emma asked when she answered the phone.

"Yes, but there's a slight change of plans," I said. "Do you want to help rescue a mystery creature?" I quickly filled her in on Thuy's phone call and the strange-looking photo.

"Ooh! This sounds exciting. I'll be right over," Emma said.

Our next mission was set!

About twenty minutes later, Nolan, Emma, and I walked out to Dad's car. Nolan had invited his friend Isla to join us too. She biked up as we were loading the car.

I greeted her, then went to grab my gloves and a bucket out of the garage. I decided to leave my snake tongs at home. Since we were likely dealing with just a frog, I wouldn't need them.

When I came back out, Taylor, my neighbor and friend, was standing out front. She was walking her puppy, Marshmallow.

"Are you on a snake job?" Taylor called. She didn't move from her spot on the sidewalk.

I wasn't surprised Taylor kept her distance. She was scared of snakes and mostly steered clear of club business.

"Sort of," I said.

"Well, good luck!" Taylor called.

Marshmallow barked like she was wishing us luck too.

"Thanks! Let's hang out when we get back home," I said.

"Maybe we can play soccer," Emma added as she climbed into the back seat.

On the way over to Thuy's, we chatted about what kind of creature might be stuck in the dark gap.

"I've always wanted to see an alien," Isla said.

Emma grabbed her sketchbook. She carried it with her everywhere, just like I did with my snake notebook. She was a good artist and drew a quick sketch of an alien with large antennae.

Dad had no trouble finding Thuy's house. It was located close to a pond in a nearby neighborhood. Thuy was on her front porch when we arrived. She waved at us as we piled out of the car.

"Thank you for coming," Thuy said. Her voice sounded just like it had on the phone. "You were so quick too! I'll show you where the creature is stuck. I'm not so good at dealing with these sorts of things."

"We're happy to help," Dad said.

Nolan and Isla followed right behind Thuy. Dad, Emma, and I walked quickly after them. I couldn't wait to solve this mystery!

Thuy's yard backed up to a golf course. The grass was so green and thick that it was hard to tell where the golf course stopped and the yard began. A low metal fence separated them.

The grass felt springy and thick as we walked onto the patio. An overhead cover made it almost dark on the back porch. I crouched down next to Nolan and Isla. Looking at the leg-antennae thing up close, I noticed some bumps and a pattern.

"Naomi, can I borrow your gloves? I can try to pull this thing out," Nolan said.

I passed the gloves to my brother. Given how much he used to dislike snakes and reptiles, this was a big deal. When we'd first started the club, Nolan would stand far back on rescues and never touched snakes.

Is he trying to impress Isla? I wondered.

Emma held her phone out to record the moment. I noticed Nolan's hands shook a bit

as he reached forward to grab those two things sticking up. Then he paused.

"You're doing great," Dad said. "Slow and steady."

As Nolan lifted the creature, I realized I was mostly right—it was a type of frog. But that wasn't all!

CHAPTER 3

ONE MYSTERY REVEALED

Snake fact #3: A female rattlesnake carries eggs inside her body to keep them safe and at the right temperature.. After about three months, the eggs hatch inside of her and then she gives birth.

Nolan gasped as he pulled the creature free. Only it was more than one creature—a snake's mouth surrounded a toad's body!

My brother started to lift the toad-snake combo. Emma moved her phone in for a closer look.

"I think I might faint," Thuy said, sitting down in one of her patio chairs.

I leaned in closer. No wonder the picture Thuy had sent us looked weird! The middle of the toad's body looked strange with the snake's mouth around it.

The toad must have been too big for the snake to pull down into the gap. They'd just stayed there—stuck as could be.

"It's a Gulf Coast Toad," I said. I took a quick look at the snake's striped pattern. "And either a ribbon snake or a Texas patch-nosed snake. Don't worry—it's nonvenomous."

"Hold on tight!" Isla said, reaching out her hands to support the snake's body.

I grabbed the bucket, even though I wanted to be the one holding the snake. Nolan and Isla lowered the creatures inside.

"Great job," Dad said.

Emma stopped recording. "Do you think the toad is alive?"

"I'm not sure," I admitted. "Some frogs can breathe underwater for more than six hours. But I don't know if a Gulf Coast Toad can survive in a snake's mouth like that."

"There's a pond nearby. Why don't we release the pair there so things can play out as naturally as possible?" Dad said.

I nodded. I liked snakes. I liked toads too. But no matter what, snakes needed to eat to survive. They kept an importance balance in the ecosystem. And like Mom always said, we had to let nature do its thing.

I leaned in to look at the bucket. Now that I could see the snake more clearly, I noticed the way the stripe covered the top of its head.

I thought of snake fact #84: *Texas patch-nosed snakes have a big protective scale on the tips of their snouts. The scale is how the snake got its name—it looks like a patched-on piece.*

This was definitely a Texas patch-nosed snake.

Thuy stood up. "I can't thank you enough! I'll fix the separation in my patio so no other creatures try to move in there." She held out a twenty-dollar bill to Nolan.

"That's kind of you to offer, but no thanks. We just want to help," Nolan said.

I stared at my brother in shock. Nolan was always looking to get paid—usually so he could buy more books. When we'd first started our snake-rescue club, he'd practically begged for tips!

"But if you're ever looking to hire someone for your yard, keep me in mind," he added.

That sounded more like my brother. Nolan had started a lawn mowing business after one of our rescues. We'd found a snake hiding in a neighbor's overgrown grass.

"Thank you! I will," Thuy said. She walked us over to the metal fence in her backyard. It had a gate leading to a golf course. "You can follow that trail to get to the pond."

Dad took the bucket from me as we hurried to the pond area. "I'll keep this as steady as possible," he said.

"Thanks," I said.

"I couldn't believe it when you pulled out a snake along with the toad!" Emma said. "I can't wait to post the video on our website."

Nolan groaned again. "I should've acted braver."

"You were yourself, which is a good thing," Isla said. Things were quiet for a moment, then she added, "Did you know that there are some frogs that actually eat snakes?" She told us all about a video she'd seen of a snake trying to eat a frog, but then things turned around.

"If koi sometimes eat snakes, I can believe it," I said, thinking about some recent research.

Dad cradled the bucket in his arms like he was holding a baby. "It's like what your mom says: 'Whether you eat or get eaten is sometimes a matter of size.'"

Even though it was morning, it was still hot. I was sweating by the time we got close to the water. We found a rocky, scrubby area far enough from the trail and the pond.

"Is it too dry here?" Emma asked as our feet crunched on the gravel and rocks.

I shook my head. "Texas patch-nosed snakes love the land, not the water. They usually live in brushy or rocky areas," I said. "Plus they have a large scale on their noses to keep them safe when they burrow."

Dad carefully set the bucket down.

"Can I be the one to release it?" Isla asked. Nolan handed her the gloves.

I nodded, even though I wanted to do the rescuing and releasing. *We're part of club,* I reminded myself.

Emma got her camera ready again and started to record the release. Isla's hands were steady as she picked up the snake. It still didn't let go of the toad!

"Way to go," I said as Isla carefully set the snake behind a rock.

"What do you think is going to happen, Naomi?" Emma asked.

"I guess only time will tell," I said.

We walked back on the trail, but Nolan pointed right—away from Thuy's house—instead of left.

"We're close to the pond," he said. "It's probably the some one that lady mentioned on the phone this morning. Let's see if she was right about that mean snake."

"Mean snake?" Emma said, looking around.

I filled her and Isla in on the phone call from this morning. "But the pond is big. I bet the snake is long gone by now," I finished.

"I agree with Nolan. We should take a look," Isla said.

"Fine with me," Dad said. He kept his eyes down on the trail as we walked. I wondered if he was keeping an eye out for the mean snake in an effort to keep us safe.

The water of the pond sparkled as we got close. A large red-eared slider sat on a rock, soaking up the sunshine.

"Do you think that's the turtle the couple rescued earlier?" I asked.

"It's too bad they didn't mark it with some paint or something so we'd know for sure," Isla said.

"Our mom had to help with some turtles that had been spray-painted like graffiti before," Nolan said. "They looked bright and funny, but it was actually sad. She said they couldn't get the benefits of the sun with paint on them."

I remembered how Mom said the paint could make turtles sick. Plus there was no way those painted turtles could hide from predators.

"Okay, no paint, but a tracking device would've been cool," Isla said. "Did you know some sharks at the Texas coast have tracking devices on them?"

Emma shook her head. "No, but thinking about the coast makes me want to go to the beach. But maybe not in the water if there are sharks swimming around."

"Agreed! The beach sounds so fun. I've always wanted to see a sea turtle hatchling release," I said.

Mom had shared pictures from one of her work trips where she'd helped release baby Kemp's ridley sea turtles. They had the tiniest little flippers!

Just then a familiar voice interrupted my thoughts. "Naomi! Emma! Over here!"

CHAPTER 4

MISSING TORTOISE

Snake fact #4: Sea snakes (like the turtle-headed sea snake) and water snakes (like the banded water snake) spend most of their lives near the water. They give birth to live babies.

Mario Orteaga, a kid from school, waved at us from a wooden dock. He was going into fourth grade at Austin Bats Elementary with Emma, Taylor, and me.

"Hey!" I called out as we made our way over.

"Have you rescued any more snakes recently?" Mr. Orteaga asked us.

The Orteaga family had been one of our club's first rescues. We'd helped a snake that had gotten trapped in their pool skimmer cover.

"We just dropped off a Texas patch-nosed snake," Nolan said.

Emma showed Mario and his dad the videos she'd taken on her phone.

"Cool! I can't believe it had a toad in its mouth like that," Mario said.

"I know!" I said. "Have *you* caught anything good?"

Mario shook his head. "Not yet. One of the guys out here earlier caught a bluegill, but he said there's a mean snake around too. He throws whatever he catches at it so it will leave him alone."

A mean snake? That has to be the same one the couple told me about, I thought.

"Did he say where he saw the snake or what it looks like?" I asked.

Mario shook his head again. "No, sorry," he said.

Nolan looked over the edge of the dock like he was searching for the snake.

"You think there's really a mean snake?" Emma asked.

I looked around. "There must be something going on. Snakes aren't mean on purpose."

"We're planning to be out here again tomorrow morning," Mario said. "I'll see what I can find out."

"That would be great," I said. We needed more information.

Before we walked back to the car, we checked to see see if there were any signs of the Texas patch-nosed snake and the toad. They were both gone.

"Do you think the toad was lunch, or do you think it was able to get away?" Isla asked.

I was just about to answer when Nolan said, "Either way, I have a feeling that things played out the way they were supposed to."

"Good answer," Dad responded, jingling the car keys in his pocket. "I'd consider this mission a success."

Me too, I thought. *I just hope we can solve the mystery of the mean snake next.*

When Dad pulled back into our driveway, Taylor and Marshmallow came running over. Taylor was yelling something, but I couldn't hear her from inside the car.

I flung open the door as soon as I could. "Are you or Marshmallow hurt?"

"We're fine," Taylor said. "But on our walk, we met a family searching for their pet tortoise. I promised the family the club would help."

"A tortoise?" Emma asked. She slid out of the back seat followed by Isla. Nolan nearly tripped as he got out of the front seat.

Taylor pulled a slip of paper out of her pocket. "I came home to write down the family's address while I waited for y'all to get back. I took some notes too. It's a sulcata tortoise, whatever that means. He got out of an open gate. He's eight pounds. His name is Thunderdome."

"That's the perfect name for a tortoise," Isla said. "I always wanted one for a pet, but my parents said no. They can grow to be more than a hundred pounds."

"I bet it would take a lot to feed a tortoise when it gets that big. I want to eat all the time, and I'm not even a hundred pounds yet," Nolan said. He reached down and gave Marshmallow a rubdown.

I wanted a pet snake, but a pet tortoise would be neat too. I knew from Mom that they could have fun personalities.

I turned to Taylor. "Did you get any more information about Thunderdome?"

Taylor looked back at her notes. "He got out of the fence at the corner of Lantana Drive and Bluebonnet Lane."

"Do you think Thunderdome ended up at the pond?" I asked, thinking of the phone call from that morning.

It was possible the turtle the woman had found was actually a tortoise. Most people didn't know the difference. I should've asked her where she'd found it or gotten her information.

"I bet we would've noticed a tortoise. We were just there," Isla said.

"The pond is a pretty big place," I said. Then a terrible thought popped into my mind. "What if that couple tossed the tortoise in the water thinking they were saving it?"

"Would that be bad?" Taylor asked, looking confused.

I nodded. "Tortoises have shells and legs built for land, not for swimming. If he got tossed into the water, he might've sunk to the bottom."

"I don't think anyone would just throw him into the pond," Nolan said. "Besides, the phone call about the turtle might not have anything to do with the missing tortoise."

"I hope you're right," I said. But I had my doubts.

Emma pulled up a picture of a sulcata tortoise on her phone. She did a quick sketch in her notebook. "We should make 'missing tortoise' signs to hang up around the neighborhood."

"Great idea! That's something I can help with," Taylor said.

Emma wrote above the sketch. *Thunderdome is missing! If found, call our club.* She added our phone number.

"I'll go make copies," Taylor said. She turned and headed across the street with Emma's sketch in hand.

Nolan groaned. "Now we'll have even more phone calls."

"It'll be worth it if we can bring Thunderdome home and help any other critters. Dad, can we help hang up missing signs and look for Thunderdome?" I asked.

Dad looked over from where he was rinsing out the bucket at the outside faucet. "Yes, but please stay close to the neighborhood," he said. "I don't want you roaming around the pond without me."

We nodded in agreement.

When Dad put the bucket up, he started singing to himself. "Bring Thunderdome home. Bring Thunderdome home!"

I laughed, then followed Emma, Nolan, and Isla inside our house. We all washed up, then grabbed snacks and water. With all of the excitement of the morning, I hadn't had anything since the smoothie.

Soon we were ready to start searching for Thunderdome. But before we could, there was a slight change in plans.

CHAPTER 5

A NEW PATIENT

Snake fact #5: Green anacondas give birth to live young, sometimes even underwater! The babies grow attached to a yolk sack that's surrounded by a membrane.

Mom pulled into the driveway, parked the car, and climbed out holding a carrier.

"Say hello to our newest patient," she greeted us.

I felt like a vet in training when Mom brought animals home to help. I wanted to be a vet just like her. I loved when the animals got well enough to release back into nature, even if it was tough. I always got so attached.

When I looked inside the carrier, l noticed bits of red, yellow, and black. I was almost positive it was a milk snake.

It's so pretty, I thought.

"I can carry that for you," Nolan offered.

"Sure, but please be careful. This gal has several broken vertebrae," Mom said as she gathered her purse.

Poor thing! Nolan lifted up the carrier gently. Isla and Emma peeked inside.

"Whoa!" Isla said. "How does the rhyme go? 'Red and yellow, kill a fellow. Red and black, friend of Jack.' This one is a friend and not a coral snake, right?"

Mom nodded. "That's right, but that rhyme isn't always accurate. Some nonvenomous snakes, like the long-nosed snake, have red and yellow touching together. Plus coral snakes can have different color patterns."

"And coral snakes might be venomous, but they're shy and friends of the environment at least," I added.

We made our way back inside our house. Nolan set the carrier down on our coffee table near the empty terrarium.

"Instead of the rhyme, I like to think of red-and-yellow patterns as stoplight colors. They encourage people to be cautious," Mom continued. She took off her shoes and placed her purse on a hook.

I made a mental note to add the tip to my notebook later. It could go near snake fact #101: *There are more than 100 types of coral snakes! These are small, shy, colorful snakes related to cobras.*

"Need anything?" Dad asked as he joined us in the living room.

"How about some paper towels to line the terrarium?" Mom said.

Dad dashed to the kitchen to grab a whole roll of paper towels. I helped him line the bottom of the terrarium.

"We'll have to keep things simple inside the terrarium while the snake heals," Mom said. "We want avoid any falls or extra pressure on the broken bones."

As we all watched, she carefully pulled the snake out of the carrier. The snake had bright red, yellow, and black bands.

"It's definitely a milk snake!" I said now that I could get a better look.

"I never thought I'd say this about a snake, but it's beautiful," Emma said.

If we didn't have the tortoise to search for, I had a feeling she would've started drawing a picture of the snake right then and there.

Isla leaned closer to look at the snake. There was a kink in its back along with some swelling.

"Do you how she got hurt?" Isla asked.

Mom shook her head. "One of my patients discovered her on a trail east of here and brought her into the clinic. She has a lot of healing to do. Hopefully she'll eventually be able to move and eat without problems."

We watched as Mom gently set the snake into the terrarium. Then she added a plastic box with an opening for the snake to hide in. The snake didn't move.

"Is she okay?" I asked.

"She'll be slow for a while. We'll work on pain control while she heals." Mom pulled a folder out of her bag.

"Let me guess—you're about to show us some X-rays?" Nolan asked.

"You know me too well." Mom held up an image of the snake's spine. There was a dark-looking area between the white bones.

Emma pointed to the dark space. "Is that the broken part?"

Mom motioned to the swollen spot on the snake. "Yes, that's the area right there," she said.

Isla twisted her arm to rub along her own spine. "Ouch," she said.

I winced just thinking about it. "I'm glad someone cared enough to help the snake."

"Me too—" Mom started to say, but then there was a knock on our front door.

"That must be Taylor," I realized. "She's waiting on us."

"We're supposed to be hanging up some signs for a missing tortoise," Nolan explained as I went to answer the door.

It *was* Taylor, along with Marshmallow on a leash. Taylor looked over at everyone standing by the terrarium.

"Sorry for the delay!" I said. Taylor might be afraid of snakes, but I didn't want her to feel left out. "My mom brought a milk snake home to rehabilitate right as we were heading over to your place. Do you want to come in and meet her?"

Taylor stared over at the terrarium with wide eyes. Marshmallow pulled at the leash to come inside, but Taylor tugged her back.

"Uh, maybe some other time," she said. "Are you ready?"

Mom smiled. "You all go on ahead. We've done everything we can for the snake at this point."

I wanted to stick around and ask more questions, but we still had a mystery to solve. Time was ticking to find the tortoise.

"See you soon!" I told my parents.

We headed out of the house. Taylor passed out posters and some painter's tape.

"Where should we go first?" she asked, holding Marshmallow's leash. The puppy was sniffing all over.

"Maybe over to the community message board by the park and then close to where the tortoise got out," Isla suggested.

"Let's split into two groups. We can cover more ground that way," Nolan said. "Isla, you and I should head to Lantana Drive. Naomi, Emma, and Taylor, why don't you all hang up some signs on the community message board at the park? Let's meet back on our street in about thirty minutes."

"Sure," Isla said. Then we separated.

"How fast do you think a tortoise could travel?" Emma asked as we made our way down the street.

I helped Taylor hang a sign on the side of a mailbox on our street. "I remember reading that some turtles can travel a mile an hour," I said.

"Do you think we could train Marshmallow to be a search-and-rescue dog for other animals?" Taylor asked. "That would be helpful."

"She's a smart puppy, so maybe," I said. We'd had some luck training her to avoid snakes.

When we reached the park, the message board was full of business cards and flyers. Emma and I rearranged some of the cards so there was space for the missing tortoise sign.

A little boy playing at the park came over to meet Marshmallow. Taylor pointed to the sign we'd just hung up.

"If you see a tortoise that looks like this, tell your parents to call us, okay?" Taylor said.

The little boy nodded and ran off to climb on the equipment.

We hung up several more missing signs around the neighborhood. I looked around near the hedges and fences too. A tortoise could be good at hiding and blending in. That's when I noticed something round sticking out from a shrub in someone's yard.

"Look over there!" I said.

CHAPTER 6

A SIGHTING

Snake fact #6: Female snakes lay a group of eggs called a clutch. The average clutch can have five to thirty eggs depending on the snake species. Large snakes, like reticulated pythons and Burmese pythons, can lay close to one hundred eggs!

Emma ran to the overgrown shrub. "Is that what I think it is?"

Taylor joined her. Marshmallow's tail wagged, and the puppy pawed through the shrub's leaves at what looked like the dome of a tortoise shell.

"Careful, Marshmallow," Taylor warned.

Marshmallow pawed it again, and the dome thing moved. I caught my breath. We'd done it! We'd found Thunderdome!

Our club is great at solving mysteries, I thought proudly.

But then the object rolled toward us. It was a camouflage-colored soccer ball.

Emma let out a disappointed sigh. "I really thought it was a tortoise," she said, rolling the ball right back to where we'd found it.

Just then an older woman came outside. "What are you all doing out in my yard?" she yelled, hurrying toward us.

A look came over her face like she recognized us. "You're those snake kids! I've seen you walking around the neighborhood with those snake picker-upper thingies. Is there a snake in our yard?"

I quickly shook my head. "Don't worry! We're looking for a missing tortoise." I pointed to the soccer ball sticking out of the shrub. "At first, I thought that might've been the tortoise. Sorry for walking in your yard without permission."

Emma handed over our last missing tortoise poster.

The woman calmed down. "It's okay. I guess I can see why you'd think that. I'll keep my eyes open for the turtle," she said.

I almost corrected her by saying "tortoise," but I was already so embarrassed.

Why would she listen to us when we couldn't tell the difference between a soccer ball and a tortoise? I thought.

"Thanks," I said instead.

We raced off, laughing.

"I sure hope Nolan and Isla had better luck than we did," I said as we made our way back to our street.

"Same! Want to play some tortoise-ball while we wait?" Emma asked.

"You mean soccer?" Taylor asked.

We burst out laughing again.

At home, I pulled my soccer ball out of the garage. We kicked it back and forth, which was challenging because Marshmallow kept pouncing and trying to bite the ball.

A few minutes later, Nolan and Isla rounded our street corner. They looked like they were having a serious conversation.

Did something happen to the tortoise? I worried.

As soon as they joined us, Marshmallow lost interest in the soccer ball. She greeted Nolan and Isla like she hadn't seen them in days.

"Everything okay?" I asked.

"Everything is fine. We hung up a few signs, but didn't find any clues," Nolan said. "Did you find any leads?"

"We found a tortoise-ball," I said, telling him the story.

Nolan started laughing and didn't stop for a whole minute.

I'll never hear the end of this one, I thought.

For dinner that night, Dad made one of my favorite meals—vegetable lasagna that oozed with cheese and sauce. Isla, Emma, and Taylor had all gone back home, so it was just Nolan, Mom, Dad, and me. And the milk snake too, of course, but she was in her terrarium.

"When do Naomi and I have our next eye exams?" Nolan asked while he scooped some salad into his bowl.

Mom passed Dad some garlic bread. "Not until August. Why?" she asked.

"We might want to get Naomi in sooner. She couldn't tell a soccer ball from a tortoise today," Nolan said, laughing.

"Oh, stop already," I said. I explained what had happened to Mom and Dad. "The shrub had so many leaves, and the soccer ball looked like a shell. Plus, it was a *camo*-colored soccer ball."

"Sure . . ." Nolan said.

I reached for a piece of garlic bread. It was pillowy soft inside and crusty on the outside. "Everyone agreed it looked like a tortoise," I insisted.

Mom nodded. "The scutes—or bony plates on a tortoise shell—do look an awful lot like the pattern on a soccer ball, especially if it was camo-colored," she said.

I smiled at her, grateful for the support.

After devouring dinner, I told Mom about the phone call we'd gotten early this morning. "The woman said they found and released a good-sized turtle at the pond. I think it might be the tortoise. Do you think it will be okay, especially if it's in the water?"

Mom dabbed her chin with a napkin. "Some tortoises like to soak in shallow areas. And I've heard of others floating if they get caught in deeper water. Hopefully, this tortoise is in a safe spot."

"I hope so," I said. I tried not to think about the other problems, like predators Thunderdome could run into. There were coyotes in our area that might try to snack on a tortoise.

Mom poured herself more water. "Did you know that moving a turtle—or a tortoise—too far from its territory can be a problem for survival the same way it can be for snakes?"

I shook my head and added a mental update to snake fact #279. *Moving snakes away from their resources to an unfamiliar territory can lower their chance of survival. *Same with turtles and tortoises.*

"Could a snake get rabies or something else that might make it sick and aggressive?" Nolan asked.

"Only mammals can get rabies," Mom said, starting to clean up dinner. "Why do you ask?"

"Mario told us about a report of a mean snake by the dock. That's actually why the woman called the club this morning, not about the turtle," I said.

"Interesting," Mom said. "The snake might be acting out of fear or for some other reason.

It's too dark to head to the pond now, but let's visit tomorrow after breakfast."

"Even I'd consider waking up early for that," Nolan said.

I laughed. My brother was *not* a morning person. I, on the other hand, couldn't wait. I was willing to do whatever it took to solve the mystery of the mean snake and find Thunderdome!

CHAPTER 7

MOO

Snake fact #7: After laying eggs, most snakes don't stick around. Southern African pythons are different—they wrap around their eggs after basking in the sun.

After dinner, Nolan and I helped wash and dry the dishes. Then we all gathered in the living room. Dad searched for a movie for us to watch, which always seemed to take forever.

I decided to check on the milk snake in the meantime. She was in the box hiding. I took that as a good sign—it meant she was able to move.

The snake needed a name while she was here recovering. "What do you guys think about calling her Leche or Moo?" I asked my family. "She *is* a milk snake."

Nolan looked over at the terrarium. "I like the name Moo even if I have no idea why a milk snake is called a milk snake."

"Some folks used to think milk snakes milked cows or drank milk because they were often found in barns and other areas where cows were kept," Mom explained. "But the truth is, they're drawn to those areas because of a different food source—mice."

I added that fact to my notebook:

Snake fact #294: Milk snakes hang out in barns, and people used to think they drank milk instead of eating mice.

"A snake called Moo sounds like a fun book or song title," Dad said. I thought he was going to start singing, but he kept scrolling through movie descriptions instead.

"I'll need some help giving Moo pain medication after the movie," Mom said.

"Sure thing," I said. "How long do you think it will take her to heal?"

"Months," Mom said. "We'll even need to be careful with feeding so she doesn't strain herself as she digests. We'll take it slowly and make sure she's not suffering. Moo might always have the kink in her spine and other complications."

"Does that mean Moo would stay here?" Nolan asked.

Mom sat up and straightened out a couch pillow. "It's a real possibility we might not be able to release her, but we would all need to agree on letting her stay here."

"She's a neat snake," Nolan said.

Does that mean he wants her to stay? I wondered.

I'd always wanted a pet snake, but I didn't want Moo to suffer. The best thing would be if she recovered and could go back to nature.

"I want what's best for Moo," I said.

"That's the heart of rehabilitation," Mom said. Then she turned her attention back to the screen and helped Dad finally pick out a movie.

I couldn't focus when the movie started. *Will Moo become a permanent part of our family?* I wondered. As Mom liked to say, only time would tell.

After the movie ended, Mom got the supplies ready for Moo's medication. Then she reached gently into the terrarium to pick up the milk snake.

"We're here to help you," she said calmly.

Dad held a small rectangle of plastic that looked like a credit card. He used it to try to open the snake's mouth. The snake wriggled.

"Please don't hurt yourself, Moo," Mom said in a soothing voice. "The more comfortable you are, the quicker you'll heal. Naomi, will you try to keep the snake still?"

Nolan jumped up in front of me. "I can do it."

Mom asked me, not you, I thought.

I almost started to argue, but I didn't want to scare Moo. Getting pulled out of the terrarium for medicine was stressful enough. Besides, Nolan was doing a good job. He carefully helped support Moo's body so she couldn't twist around.

"Naomi, you can try to help Dad get her mouth open," Mom said.

Dad handed me the slip of plastic.

"Open wide, just like that," I said, gently opening Moo's mouth. I wasn't afraid she would bite me. Her teeth were so teensy they would barely scratch my skin.

Dad passed Mom a syringe filled with medication. She slipped it into the back of the snake's mouth, past the glottis—the tube that connected to the windpipe. Then she pressed down on the syringe.

"Good job, everyone," Mom said as the snake swallowed the medicine. She put Moo back into the terrarium. The snake continued to stay calm.

"Get some good sleep," I said to Moo.

I was ready for bed myself. I wanted to have lots of energy for the next day. I would need it to find Thunderdome and solve the mystery of the mean snake.

The next morning, I woke up to the smell of Dad's homemade cinnamon-apple pancakes. As much as I loved Sunday breakfast, I couldn't wait to speed time along and get to the pond.

While Dad finished cooking, I checked in with Taylor and Emma. They were both planning to meet me at my house. We'd drive over to the pond with Mom and Dad.

Nolan and Isla decided to bike to the pond so Mom and Dad wouldn't have to take two vehicles. I think Nolan just wanted some independence.

We all sat down and dug into breakfast. Steam rose from the fluffy pancakes. The

apple-cinnamon flavor was perfectly sweet.
I didn't even need syrup! Just as I took a
second bite, our phone rang.

"I'm surprised we've gone this long without
a phone call," Nolan said.

"I'll get it!" I said with my mouth full.
I raced over to the phone. "Hello?"

"Is this the snake club president?" a
woman asked. Her voice was shaky, and
she talked slowly.

"Yes, ma'am," I said, certain it was the same caller as before.

"Well, I had to call back because I came across one of your posters on our morning walk. That drawing looked just like the turtle my husband and I dropped off at the pond," the woman said. "I'm sorry—I didn't know it was someone's pet. We thought we were helping."

"Your heart was in the right place," I told her. "Thank you for calling with more information."

I got her contact information and found out her name was Joanne Swanson. Then I had to know. "Do you remember if you set the tortoise in the pond water or on dry ground?"

"We left it sitting in a nice little sunny spot near some rocks," Mrs. Swanson said.

I took a deep breath. That was good news. Hopefully the tortoise had continued to stay far away from the water.

"Thank you again, Mrs. Swanson," I said.

"I really did think we were doing a good thing. I hope we can find the tortoise. My husband and I will be looking later," she said.

"We'll be searching, too. Maybe we'll see you at the pond," I said. Once I'd hung up, I told my family about the phone call. "I had a feeling Thunderdome might be hiding somewhere near the pond."

But is he still out there? I wondered.

CHAPTER 8

THE THIEF

Snake fact #8: An "egg tooth" helps a baby snake escape from its egg when it's time to hatch. This sharp bump on the end of the snake's snout eventually disappears.

Before Emma and Taylor came over, Mom, Dad, Nolan, and I pitched in to give Moo her morning pain medication.

"Let's do exactly what we did last night," Mom said as she gently pulled Moo out of the terrarium.

Everyone got into position. Mom held Moo. Nolan supported her. I helped open her mouth. Dad and Mom teamed up to squirt in the medicine.

Moo didn't fight us at all. I really hoped she knew we were trying our hardest to save her life.

Once we were done, Mom set a small, speckled egg inside the terrarium. "We'll add to her diet when we can, but this egg will be easy enough for her to digest in the meantime," she said. "Plus, she won't need to spend much effort 'hunting' it down."

I remembered what Mom had said about how much effort it would take for Moo to digest food. That would be hard to do with broken

bones and sore muscles. A small egg like this seemed like a good starting place. Moo needed food to keep up her energy so she could heal.

Moo ignored the egg and glided to her hide, flipping on her back in the process. She struggled before she could turn over onto her tummy.

"Is she okay?" I asked.

"She's struggling with coordination," Mom said. "Hopefully that's only temporary while she heals, but it might be permanent."

I hoped Moo would make a full recovery. A snake who couldn't move well wouldn't survive if we released her back into the wild. If that was the case, she would be much safer with us. We would give her a good home.

Emma arrived at my house first. "How's the milk snake doing?" she asked, peeking into the hide. "Did you name her yet?"

I smiled. "We named her Moo. She has to take medicine, and we're hoping it helps. But

Mom isn't sure if she'll ever be well enough to be released back in nature."

"That's sad, but at least Moo would have a happy life here," Emma said. She pulled out her sketchbook and did a quick drawing of the snake.

"I hope she eats soon," I said.

A few minutes later, Taylor arrived with Marshmallow.

"Are you sure you want to bring your puppy with us?" I said. "We've heard people talk about a snake at the pond."

I kept quiet about some people saying the snake was mean. That was still just a rumor.

"She'll be helpful," Taylor insisted. "We've been teaching her to avoid snakes, and you know I'll stay far, far away."

I had my doubts about Marshmallow being useful, especially when she tried nibbling on my ear in the back seat of Mom's SUV. But I knew there was no changing Taylor's mind.

Dad had gone overboard preparing a picnic lunch. He made a lot of noise as he loaded everything into the back of the car. Then he slid into the passenger seat while Mom got behind the wheel.

"Giddyap!" Emma said as Mom started driving.

"Yeehaw!" Taylor said in response.

I realized I hadn't told my friends about the latest phone call I'd gotten. I filled them in on the way to the pond.

"Mrs. Swanson said they released the tortoise in a rocky area. Hopefully, nobody else found him there and tried to 'help' get him into the water."

"That reminds me," Mom said from the front seat. "I remembered a case about a tortoise that had been missing for two days. Someone found it at the bottom of a small pond. It wasn't responsive, but after warming up and getting help breathing, the tortoise made a full recovery." She made a turn past the golf course to get to the pond.

That made me feel encouraged.

We arrived minutes later. Emma, Taylor, and I all piled out of the back seat. We decided to walk Marshmallow while we waited for Nolan and Isla to arrive.

In the distance, I could see Mario and his dad fishing on the dock. I couldn't wait to find out if they'd heard any reports about the tortoise or the mean snake.

Marshmallow sniffed around and nibbled on some dried grass. I looked around to see if I could find Thunderdome. Then I heard laughter. I looked up to see Nolan and Isla quickly pedaling on their bikes toward us. Isla was in the lead.

"I trust that you were both being careful?" Dad asked.

Nolan took off his bike helmet and nodded his head.

"Let's get to the dock," I said. "I want to talk to Mario."

I led the way with Emma, Taylor, Nolan, and Isla following after. As we got closer to the dock, Marshmallow's tail started wagging. She tugged at the leash to get to Mario and his dad.

"Slow down, Marshmallow!" Taylor said, running to keep up.

Mario set down his fishing pole to greet the puppy. Marshmallow gave him lots of kisses, then wiggled her way over to say hello to Mr. Orteaga.

"Your dog is sweet, Taylor," Mario said.

Taylor beamed. "She needs some more training, but she's a fast learner. I think she could even be a search-and-rescue dog."

Just then Mario's fishing pole started sliding toward the edge of the dock.

"Mario, check out your fishing pole! I think you caught something," Nolan hollered.

Mario lunged for the pole before it went over the edge. The end of the rod bent as he tried to reel in whatever was on the end of his line.

"What did you catch?" Isla asked.

A fish with whiskers splashed to the surface of the pond. "Looks like a catfish," Mario said.

"Yeah, it does. A good-sized one!" said Mr. Orteaga.

Emma pulled out her phone and started recording.

The catfish tugged at Mario's line. Suddenly a snake swam out on the surface of the water in surprise attack mode.

Taylor gasped. "That water moccasin is going to steal your fish!"

I recognized the diamond-shaped blotches on the snake's back and sides. The pattern almost looked a chain-link fence.

"It's a diamondback water snake, not a venomous water moccasin," I said.

The diamondback water snake latched onto the catfish. Mario's fishing pole was really bending now in a fishing tug-of-war.

The snake seemed determined to win. As we watched, it grabbed the catfish, which broke free of the hook. The snake started to swim off with its free meal. But the catfish wasn't giving up easily. It splashed its tail before both creatures disappeared underwater.

Whoa! Was that the 'mean' snake from the reports? I thought.

"I seriously can't believe what just happened," Isla said, peering over the edge of the dock.

I joined her trying to find where the snake went. Both it and the catfish seemed to have vanished.

"I got the whole thing on video," Emma said, looking at the screen on her phone.

The whole group—adults and kids—burst into chatter over what just happened.

"The snake had to be as long as some of you kids are tall," Nolan said.

"There have been reports of a mean snake around here. I bet that was it," I said.

Taylor shuddered. "Mean snake?"

"I guess a snake might seem mean if it's defensive or trying to get an easy meal. But snakes don't do mean things on purpose," I reminded her.

Mario chuckled. "I think that the snake needed that catfish more than me."

"The diamondback water snake seems to have become an opportunistic feeder," Mom said in her vet tone of voice. "That means it's found creative ways to get food. We'll have to look into the case further so there aren't more problems at the pond."

Taylor shuddered again. "This snake stuff is too much for me right now. Can we go look for Thunderdome?" She reached down to pull a stick out of Marshmallow's mouth.

Snake stuff was never too much for me, but I wanted to respect my friend's wishes. Besides, I wanted to search for Thunderdome too. We'd solved one problem at the pond, but the tortoise was still out there somewhere.

CHAPTER 9

THE SEARCH FOR THUNDERDOME

Snake fact #9: A baby snake is called a snakelet.

"Do you want to join us, Mario?" I asked.

Mario looked over at his dad. "Thanks, but I think we'll find a different spot to fish. Let us know if you need any help, though. We'll keep our eyes out for the tortoise—and the snake."

I smiled. "Hope you catch something great."

"Yeah, besides a hungry snake," Isla said. Nolan laughed at her joke.

We set off to explore the pond area. Mom and Dad grouped together while Nolan paired off with Isla.

I hung out with Emma and Taylor. Marshmallow started sniffing and tugged Taylor off the path. Then she started barking hysterically. Tall grass and reeds swayed, and it sounded like some twigs snapped.

"Something's wrong," Taylor said. She moved closer to Emma and me. "Do you think it's the mean snake coming after us?"

"The diamondback water snake probably has a full belly by now," I said. But even I

jumped back a little when a crunching noise sounded.

Marshmallow barked again.

"It's okay," Taylor said. But her voice sounded like things were far from okay.

Nolan and Isla came closer to see what was going on.

"I think there's some kind of animal walking in the reeds," Isla said.

"Do you think it could be an alligator? People dump them or floods bring them from east Texas," Nolan said.

Mom and Dad overheard that and came over too.

"It's unlikely," Mom said. "There would've been lots of report if there were an alligator hanging out at a neighborhood pond."

"Why don't you all step back just in case?" Dad said.

We did just that. There was another crunch, then a rustle.

"That sounds like a deer," Isla said.

"Or something bigger," Nolan added.

Just then a shadowy figure stepped out of the thick brush and reeds. Taylor covered her mouth as she yelped. Marshmallow stopped barking and wagged her tail instead.

"Sorry to give you a fright," an older man said. "My wife and I are looking for a tortoise. We should've never brought it here in the first place."

"Are you Mrs. Swanson's husband?" I asked.

The old man smiled and held out his hand. "I sure am. The name's Harold Swanson. You must be the snake club! Joanne's on the other side of the pond looking. I know she would love to meet you all in person."

Mr. Swanson joined our search party, and we headed in the direction of where Mrs. Swanson was looking for Thunderdome.

Emma slowed down to take a couple pictures of some interesting rocks close to the trail.

Isla picked up a rock with layers in the shape of an ear. "This is a fossilized oyster."

"Nice find," Nolan said. "Crazy to think how this area was all underwater during ancient times."

Nolan and Isla scoped out the area for fossils while the adults chatted. That's when something caught my eye. Past the rocks, closer to the bank, was a spot that had been dug out. It looked like a tiny cove.

I pointed to the area. "That looks like a den of some sort."

"I can't see too well from this angle, but it could be a nutria den or home to some kind of reptile," Mom said.

Taylor jumped back. "What's a nutria?" she asked.

"It's a large rodent that lives around the water," Mom replied. "Some people mistake it for an otter or a big guinea pig."

Marshmallow started pulling Taylor toward the cove. The puppy barked, and something moved in the brush. It looked kind of like the camouflaged soccer ball from before.

"That could be Thunderdome," I said.

"I'll check it out," Nolan offered, racing over to the cove.

Isla hurried after him, and they started moving some dirt out of the way. I saw something that looked like a thick leg covered in overlapping scales.

A moment later, Nolan plucked out a reptile with a large dome.

"Thunderdome!" I cried.

Emma recorded the whole thing.

"That's definitely a sulcata tortoise," Mom said. "I don't have a scale on me, but I'd say he weighs right about eight pounds." She checked him out all over. "Thunderdome is in great shape. He must've been saving up energy and finding a place to stay cool to avoid overheating."

This made me think of snake fact #58: *Snakes and other reptiles are cold-blooded. They rely on their surroundings to control their body temperature.*

Taylor cheered. "Good job helping us find the tortoise, Marshmallow."

I wanted to protest that I'd noticed the cove first—before Marshmallow had pulled Taylor in that direction. But I reminded myself that credit for the rescue didn't matter.

We're a team. The important thing is that Thunderdome is safe and will be heading back home to the family who misses him, I thought.

"I had no idea how exciting this day would be," Mr. Swanson said.

"Goodness, me neither," Mr. Swanson said.

Nolan carried Thunderdome for a bit as we rounded the trail to find Mrs. Swanson. It looked like he was holding a giant sandwich in his hands.

We finally found Mrs. Swanson on the trail. She smiled so wide it had to hurt her face.

"That's him! That's the tortoise we found in the road!" she exclaimed. "I can't thank you all enough. I'll make sure to let everyone know how wonderful your snake club is."

"Thank you," I said. "We also solved the mystery of the mean snake you saw. It's not mean at all. It's just gotten used to people feeding it. I bet it thought you had a treat for it to steal when you were carrying the tortoise."

"Well, I'll be," Mrs. Swanson said. "Our neighborhood is lucky to have you kids."

As we walked back to our car, we passed the dock. Mario came running over.

"You found the tortoise!" he exclaimed.

Even Mr. Orteaga came over to check out Thunderdome. "The snake club looks out for critters of all kinds. That's really impressive!"

"I couldn't agree more," Mom said, beaming proudly.

"This mission has made me hungry," Dad said. "Who's up for a picnic?

He retrieved the cooler and snacks from the car, and we had a giant picnic party with everyone at the pond. With Mom's permission, I fed Thunderdome some carrot sticks. He used his beak to break off bites to crunch.

"By the way," Mario said around bites of a cheese sandwich, "we didn't see the snake again."

"I guess that's a good thing," I said, digging into my lunch too. We might have solved the mystery, but we'd still have to come up with a plan to keep the snake out of trouble.

CHAPTER 10

THE MISSION CONTINUES

Snake fact #10: Some snakes look different when they're young. Baby cottonmouths and copperheads can have green or yellow tail tips to lure prey. As they age, their tails change to look more like the adult pattern. Green pythons may start their lives either red or yellow and then change to emerald green as a way to survive different habitats.

After we finished our picnic and said our goodbyes, it was time to reunite Thunderdome with his family.

"I don't have his family's phone number, but I have my note with their address," Taylor said. She pulled a crumpled piece of paper out of her pocket.

"Why don't we drive by the house to see if anyone is home?" Dad suggested.

Mom nodded. "Sounds like a plan. I'll keep Thunderdome up front with me since Marshmallow will be in the back seat."

"Ooh, that means I get to drive your SUV," Dad said, laughing as he got behind the wheel.

Nolan and Isla got on their bikes. They would meet us at Thunderdome's family's house.

When we all got there, I rang the doorbell, holding Thunderdome in my arms. No one came out. A minute or so passed by.

Maybe we should take Thunderdome home with us for now, I thought.

But seconds later, a young girl opened the door. As soon as she saw the tortoise, she yelled, "Thunderdome!" and burst out of the house. A teenage boy followed a moment later.

"Thunderdome, you're alive!" the girl cried.

Reptiles might be cold-blooded but not cold-hearted. As soon as he saw his family, Thunderdome's legs kicked as if he was excited. Mom could barely hold him. She let the tortoise

down on the grass, and he walked right over to the girl and boy like he recognized them.

"Thanks for bringing him home," the teenager said to us.

A woman joined the two kids. "We can't thank you enough!" She pulled money out of a wallet and held it out to us. "We have a reward for you all."

"This moment is our reward," Nolan said. Isla looked over at Nolan and smiled, though I'm not sure if he noticed it or not.

I didn't have any words. It was the best feeling to watch Thunderdome be reunited with his family. The tortoise touched his nose to the little girl's arm like he felt safe and happy.

"We'll make sure to pay things forward then," the woman said, bending down to scoop Thunderdome up. She kissed him on the top of the head the same way I'd seen Taylor kiss Marshmallow. "We'll also make sure this guy doesn't get out of our gate again. Thank you!"

"Thunderdome is home! Thunderdome is home," Dad sang on the way back to our house. It was so catchy that all of us sang another round together.

"Marshmallow and I had better head home now," Taylor said when we pulled into the driveway.

Part of me wondered if Taylor didn't want to come inside because of the milk snake. Moo was safe in the terrarium and not going anywhere with her injury, but we *had* gone through a snake escape in our house before.

I nodded and waved. "Bye, Taylor! See you soon."

"I better get going too. Let me know what's going on this week," Isla said.

Nolan gave her a fist-bump. "Who knows what kind of animal we might be saving then."

Isla laughed and got on her bike to head home. Then Nolan, Emma, and I helped Dad carry the cooler to our house so we could unpack and clean it out. There wasn't much left in the cooler after our picnic with so many extra guests.

My skin pinched from all of the sunshine, but I felt even warmer on the inside. We'd found Thunderdome and safely returned him home. And when I checked on Moo, the speckled egg was gone! The snake was resting out of her hide. Her eyes looked bright, and I felt hopeful that she would recover.

No matter what, she'll have a safe place with us—a home, I thought.

The only mystery that remained was what to do about the diamondback water snake.

"Mom, what did you have in mind when you said that we should get a plan together for the snake at the pond?" I asked.

Mom washed her hands. "It should probably be relocated before someone hurts it. We should also discourage folks from feeding it."

"What if we make a sign?" I suggested.

"I can help with that," Emma said.

Dad fetched an old garage sale sign from the garage. "You girls can paint over this," he said. He handed us the sign and some waterproof acrylic paints.

We painted the sign, and Emma outlined the words, *Do not feed the snake!* in block letters. Then she drew a picture of the diamondback water snake eating a fish with a line through it.

Before we had a chance to finish filling in the letters, Emma's phone dinged. "My mom

wants to me head to the store with her," she said, reading the message. "I better get going too. Sorry I can't stay to finish our sign."

"You did the hard part, and I can take care of the rest. Thanks for your help today and always," I said.

Emma hugged me. "I love being part of something so special!"

My art skills weren't as good as Emma's, but I painted the letters. As soon as the paint was dry, I found Mom and Dad in the kitchen.

"Can we go hang our sign by the dock?" I asked.

"Ooh, I want to come too!" Nolan said.

We gathered a bucket and snake tongs, then headed for the pond. No one was there when we arrived. The afternoon sun was blazing hot. Even the fish in the pond probably thought it was too hot to be doing anything.

Dad and Nolan pushed the painted garage sale sign into the ground. After, Mom tossed a pebble into the pond like she was throwing in a fishing line. Either the snake wasn't fooled or else it was too full from earlier because there was no trace of it.

"We'll have to try relocating the snake another time," Mom said. "The sign is a good start, though."

When we got home, there were two messages on our answering machine. One was from Emma.

"Hey, guys!" she said. "Check out our website when you get a chance. My mom helped me upload some videos."

The second phone call was about snake business. "Hi, there," a guy's voice said. "My name is Arthur, and when I went up into my attic, I found a snake skin stuck to a wooden bar. Do you think you could help me identify it?" He left his contact information before hanging up.

"I bet it's a rat snake," Nolan guessed.

Rat snakes were acrobats and could get up into high places, so I had a feeling my brother was right.

"We'd better call him back for more information, but can we check our website first?" I asked.

Dad loaded it up on the family computer, and we crowded around the screen. There was a new glowing review from Thunderdome's family!

Mom read it out loud. "Our family is complete again thanks to the efforts of this great group! Fifteen out of ten rating."

Emma had uploaded a couple of short videos: the Texas patch-nosed snake rescue and Thunderdome's rescue. She'd also posted the clip of the snake snatching the catfish.

"Don't worry—this snake isn't mean. It is just taking advantage of free food. Let wildlife be wild, and please don't feed it or try to harm it," she said on the video.

"Whoa!" Nolan said. "This video already has hundreds of hits! I guess we'd better get used to more and more phone calls."

Emma and her mom are amazing! I thought. I couldn't wait to tell her that later.

"When you first mentioned starting the club, we had no idea how popular it would become. You all are making such a difference not only for animals, but for our community and beyond. Keep up the great work!" Mom said.

She squeezed me and kissed the top of my head. Nolan ducked at first when Mom tried to hug him, but then he laughed and gave in.

"We save snakes, and saving snakes we shall continue," Dad said in a pirate voice.

I grinned at my family. Dad was right. We had no plans of stopping our mission anytime soon!

GLOSSARY

aggressive (uh-GREH-siv)—ready to attack

amphibian (am-FI-bee-uhn)—a cold-blooded animal with a backbone; amphibians live in water when young and can live on land as adults

antenna (an-TE-nuh)—a feeler on an insect's head

fossil (FAH-suhl)—the remains or traces of plants and animals that are preserved as rock

hatchling (HACH-ling)—a recently hatched animal

membrane (MEM-breyn)—a thin, soft, flexible layer of animal or plant tissue

nutria (NOO-tree-uh)—a large, semi-aquatic rodent from South American

opportunistic (op-er-too-NIS-tik)—feeding on whatever food is available

rehabilitate (ree-huh-BIL-uh-tayt)—to return to health or activity

reptile (REP-tile)—a cold-blooded animal that breathes air and has a backbone; most reptiles lay eggs and have scaly skin

scute (SKOOT)—a large, flat scale on the underside of a snake

terrarium (tuh-RER-ee-uhm)—a glass or plastic container for raising land animals

venomous (VEN-uhm-us)—able to produce a poison called venom

TALK ABOUT IT!

1. How do Naomi and her family solve the mystery of the mean snake? Look back through this story to find clues. What do you think will eventually happen with the diamondback water snake?

2. Thunderdome's family is relieved to have him back. Have you ever lost something important to you? Discuss what happened. Did you get that thing back? If so, how?

3. How does Naomi remember to share the moment with others during rescues? Look back through the story to find examples. Then talk about a time you shared a moment (or something important) with someone else.

WRITE ABOUT IT!

1. There are lots of different creatures mentioned in this book. Choose your favorite, then research and write more about that animal. You can also draw a picture of the animal.

2. Naomi cares about Moo, even though the milk snake isn't officially her pet. Write about an animal you share a special bond with. If you don't have any pets, use your imagination!

3. What do you think happened to Thunderdome after he escaped from his yard? Write 2 to 3 paragraphs describing his journey from the time he got out to the time he was discovered.

SNAKE (AND TURTLE) SAFETY

It's possible you might see a snake while out playing or exploring. If you do see one, give it space. If you step on a snake or find that you are very close, move away quickly. Snakes are more likely to bite if they feel threatened. Before biting, snakes may give warning signs, including hissing, rattling (not just rattlesnakes!), or striking. They might also flatten their heads, curl into an *S* shape, or play dead.

Pay attention to these signs to prevent bites. Don't handle any snake unless you can correctly identify that it is nonvenomous. Remember, leave the snake alone, and it will leave you alone.

Turtles and tortoises are different creatures with different needs. If you find a tortoise in your neighborhood, it's likely a pet that got loose. If you find a turtle crossing the street, stay safe and watch out for any vehicles. Ask an adult to help move the turtle to safety in the direction it was moving.

For more details, check out The Orianne Society's website: oriannesociety.org/faces-of-the-forest/why-turtles-cross-roads-and-how-to-help

Research and learn more about snakes and other animals in your area by checking out field guides and books from your local library. You can also visit these websites to learn more about the animals featured in the story:

- *Campus Biodiversity: Gulf Coast Toad* biodiversity.utexas.edu/news/entry/campus-biodiversity-gulf-coast-toad
- *Fun Milk Snake Facts for Kids* kidadl.com/facts/animals/milk-snake-facts
- *Fun Patch-Nosed Snake Facts for Kids* kidadl.com/facts/animals/patch-nosed-snake-facts
- *Kids Animal Facts: Red Eared Slider Turtle Facts for Kids* kidsanimalsfacts.com/red-eared-slider-turtle-facts-for-kids
- *Maryland Zoo: Sulcata Tortoise* marylandzoo.org/animal/sulcata-tortoise

NAOMI'S TOP SNAKE FACTS

1. "Gravid" means a snake is pregnant or full of eggs.

2. Most snakes lay eggs, but some give birth to live babies the same way that mammals do.

3. A female rattlesnake carries eggs inside her body to keep them safe and at the right temperature. After about three months, the eggs hatch inside of her and then she gives birth.

4. Sea snakes (like the turtle-headed sea snake) and water snakes (like the banded water snake) live near the water most of their lives. They give birth to live babies.

5. Green anacondas give birth to live young, sometimes even underwater! The babies grow attached to a yolk sack that's surrounded by a membrane.

6. Female snakes lay a group of eggs called a clutch. The average clutch can have five to thirty eggs depending on the snake species. Large snakes, like reticulated pythons and Burmese pythons, can lay close to one hundred eggs!

ABOUT THE AUTHOR

Jessica Lee Anderson is the author of more than 50 books for children. When not writing, she enjoys exploring nature and going on hikes with her husband, Michael, and their daughter, Ava. They've come across a variety of snakes in their travels, including a rattlesnake. Jessica was once afraid of snakes, but after learning more about these unique creatures, she's developed a deep appreciation for them. You can learn more about Jessica by visiting jessicaleeanderson.com.

photo credit: Michael Anderson

ABOUT THE ILLUSTRATOR

Alejandra Barajas has a degree in fine arts from Guanajuato University, but she found her true passion in children's book illustration. She loves all kinds of stories and believes that each one has the power to teach something new and valuable. Alejandra is almost always drawing—even in her free time—but when she's not, she can be found spending time with her family and dogs in Guanajuato, Mexico.

photo credit: Alejandra Barajas

7. After laying eggs, most snakes don't stick around. Southern African pythons are different—they wrap around their eggs after basking in the sun.

8. An "egg tooth" helps a baby snake escape from its egg when it's time to hatch. This sharp bump on the end of the snake's snout eventually disappears.

9. A baby snake is called a snakelet.

10. Some snakes look different when they're young. Baby cottonmouths and copperheads can have green or yellow tail tips to lure prey. As they age, their tails change to look more like the adult pattern. Green pythons may start their lives either red or yellow and then change to emerald green as a way to survive different habitats.